THE Dancing TURTLE

AUGUST HOUSE
Little folk

A FOLKTALE FROM BRAZIL

By Pleasant DeSpain

Illustrated by David Boston

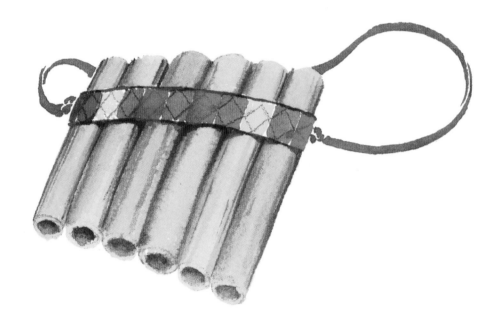

Published 1998 by August House LittleFolk
Atlanta, Georgia

Book design by Harvill Ross Studios Ltd.

Printed in South Korea
10 9 8 7 6 5 4 3 2 1

LIBRARY OF CONGRESS CATALOGING-IN-PUBLICATION DATA
DeSpain, Pleasant.
The dancing turtle: a folktale form Brazil / Pleasant DeSpain: illustrated by David Boston.
      p.   cm.
Summary: After being caught by a hunter, a clever turtle uses her wits and her talent playing
the flute to trick the hunter's children into helping her escape.
ISBN 978-1-941460-46-7 Paperback

[1. Folklore—Brazil.]   I. Boston, David, Ill.   II. Title
PZ8.1.D453Dan   1998
398.2'0981'0452792-dc21   97-38866

The paper used in this publication meets the minimum requirements of the American National
Standards for Information Sciences—permanence of Paper for Printed Library Materials,
ANSI.48-1984

for Tony Earl
mentor and friend

and for

Lucy Rose Parkhurst,
who likes the stories of Turtle,
with love

— P. DeS.

for Mallori, Drew, Cloie, and my Amanda

— D.B.

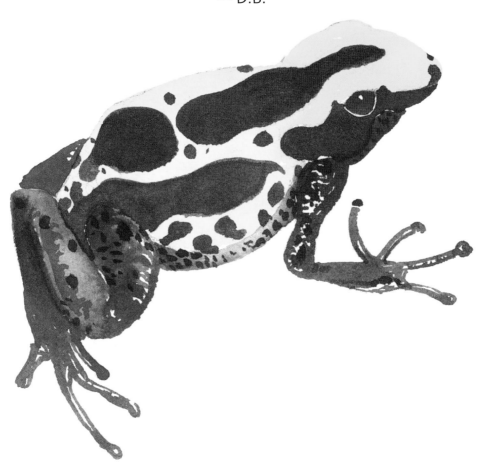

Long ago, on the bank of the mighty Amazon River,
Turtle played her flute while enjoying the sun.

She played the high notes and the low notes. She played the fast ones and the slow ones. She played her flute with such skill and joy that before long, she felt like dancing!

Turtle laid down her flute and began to dance her happiest dance. Around and around she twirled, going this way and that. She bobbed and weaved and jumped and crawled, dancing all the while.

Then she stopped. Her dance was done. She pulled her head and legs into her shell and went to sleep.

Being asleep, she didn't notice the two dark eyes of a large man peering at her from behind a broad green leaf. She didn't hear the rumble of hunger in his stomach. And she didn't feel his strong brown hand grab hold of her shell until it was too late! "Got you!" he cried. "My family will soon feast on turtle soup." He shoved Turtle and her flute into his bag and began the long walk home. It was dark by the time he arrived.

"Look at the fat turtle I've caught," he said to his two children. "I heard a flute playing in the forest and followed the sweet sounds to the edge of the river. There I saw Turtle dancing and when she finished, she went to sleep. It was easy to catch her. I'll put her in the cage, and we will make a fine soup with her tomorrow."

The man put Turtle in a cage made of strong sticks He tied the door shut. Turtle couldn't escape.

In the morning the father decided to work in the fields. He told his boy and girl, "Stay home and take care of Turtle. Don't let her out of the cage for any reason. I'll be home when the sun goes down, and we'll cook her for supper."

The man picked up his hoe and walked to the fields. While the children played near the hut, Turtle thought and thought about her difficulty.

Then she had an idea. She picked up her flute and began to play. She played the high notes and the low notes. She played the fast ones and the slow ones. She played so sweetly and so well that the girl ran to the cage and said, "play more, Turtle! Please play more!"

"I can do more than play tunes" answered Turtle. "I can dance as well."

The children had never seen a turtle dance before. The boy said, "You can't dance. Turtles can't dance. You're trying to trick us!"

"I couldn't trick you," said Turtle. "Children are too smart. All the forest animals know better than to try to trick children."

Would you try to escape if we let you out?"
asked one of the children.

"Of course not," said Turtle.
"I only want to show you how
well I can dance. But if you
don't want to see me
dance, then I'll put my
flute away and go back to sleep."

"No!" the boy cried. "You must show us."

He untied the rope, opened the door, and took
Turtle out of the cage.

Turtle played her flute. She played the high notes and the low notes. She played the fast ones and the slow ones. She played her flute with such skill and joy that she felt like dancing!

Turtle laid down her flute and began to dance her happiest dance. Around and around she twirled, going this way and that. She bobbed and weaved and jumped and crawled, dancing all the while. Then she stopped. Her dance was done.

"Again!" Cried the children. "Dance again!"

"Yes," Turtle panted, "as soon as I catch my breath. Carry me over to the shade trees, where I can cool down."

The girl picked Turtle up and carried her to the edge of the forest where the largest of the shade trees stood. "I'll take a little nap," said Turtle, "and then I'll be ready to dance again. Go and play your games. I'll play my flute when I'm rested."

After the children left, Turtle began crawling through the jungle undergrowth. She didn't rest or play her flute until she was safely home by the river. When the children grew tired of their games, they ran back to the shade trees, calling, "Turtle! Where are you, Turtle? You said you would dance for us again. Where are you hiding?"

There was no answer. Turtle had tricked them after all! Their father would be angry.

They sat on the ground and thought and thought. Soon the girl had an idea. She found a large rock shaped like Turtle's shell. She painted the rock to look just like Turtle and placed it in the cage. The boy tied the door with the rope, and the children hoped for the best.

Their hungry father arrived home as the sunlight was fading. He put a pot of water on the fire and waited for it to boil. Then he opened the cage and pulled the rock from inside.

"Turtle is still asleep," he whispered to his children, "and she weighs more than I remember."

He plopped the painted stone into the pot. "Bring the big serving plate," he said, "the one made of hard clay. It will soon be time to eat."

The children were frightened, but said nothing. They brought the plate and set it before their father. He took the rock from the pot and dropped it onto the plate. The plate broke into many pieces.

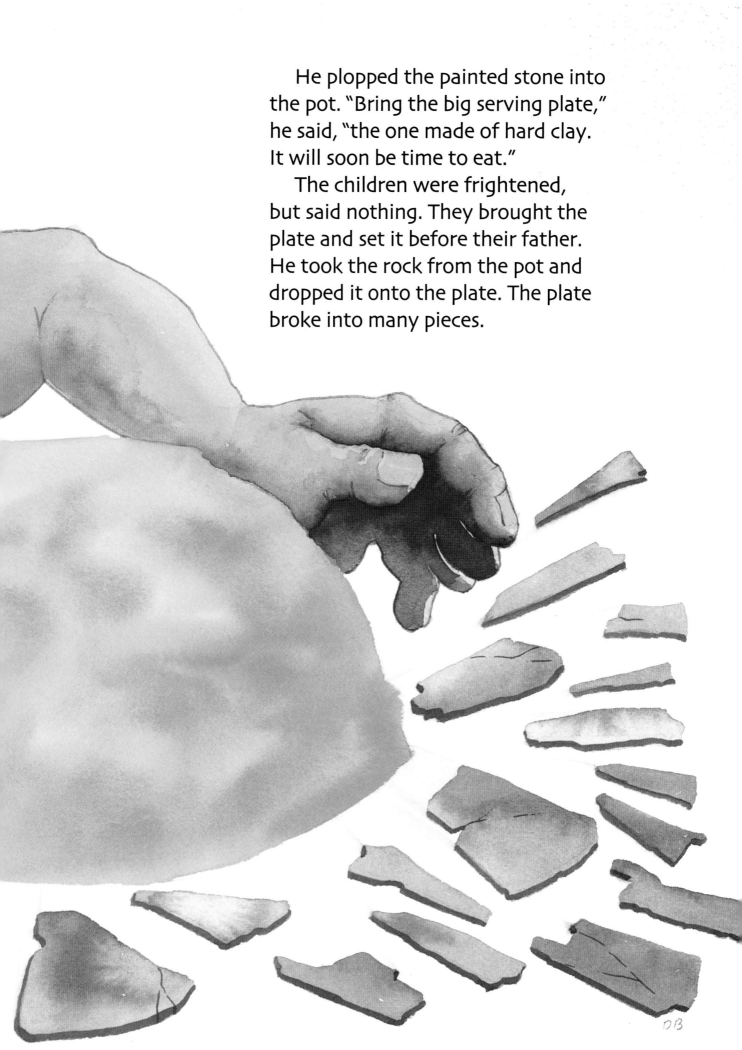

The father looked carefully at the rock.
Then he looked even more carefully at his
children.

"You let Turtle out of her cage, didn't you?"

"Yes, Father, we're sorry," said the girl.

"Turtle said she wouldn't trick us and then
she did," said the boy.

"Turtle is very clever," Father said, "more
clever than I thought. Don't worry, children.
I'll catch her again tomorrow, and then we'll
have our turtle soup."

Did he ever catch Turtle again?
What do you think?

About the Story

I love stories of Turtle from throughout the world. It is, however, the Latin American tales that most intrigue me. Like the people of Latin America, Turtle always seems to survive with courage and wit. "The Dancing Turtle" was first told by the indigenous people of Brazil, and was initially collected by José Vieira Coutode Magalhâes in O Selvagem, Rio de Janeiro, 1876. It was, of course, told by villagers for hundreds of years before 1876 and is still being told today.

A few years ago, I journeyed to the jungles of Costa Rica and Nicaragua, and asked my various guides to share a story about Turtle. It was this story–with a variety of imaginative and cultural variants–that was most often told. A fourteen-year-old Costa Rican boy named Juan Carlos, who spoke as little English as I did Spanish, acted out his version of "The Dancing Turtle" as we traveled upriver on a small and leaky boat. He perfectly pantomimed Turtle's capture and escape, and nearly tipped the boat over as he demonstrated her skill at dancing. Juan Carlos's father, who was also the boat's captain, sternly rebuked his son. Then all three of us laughed, as the story ends so very well.

I've told this tale in many schools and libraries, and the question most often asked upon its completion is: "Did Turtle really lie to the children?" I always answer truthfully and ask, "Would you tell a lie to save your life?" Nearly everyone nods or says yes.

In the ancient stories of the East, and in the more current tales of the West, Turtle symbolizes Mother Earth. Many creation myths say that Turtle carries the world on her back and thus represents nature's innate wisdom. In this time of ecological destruction and hope for resurrection, it is worth remembering Turtle's courage and wit.

— P. DeS.